go for
goal

go for goal

stories chosen by
wendy cooling

Dolphin

A Dolphin paperback

First published in Great Britain in 1997
by Orion Children's Books
a division of the Orion Publishing Group Ltd
Orion House
5 Upper St Martin's Lane
London WC2H 9EA

A catalogue record for this book is available
from the British Library
Typeset by Deltatype Ltd, Birkenhead, Merseyside
Printed in Great Britain by Clays Ltd, St Ives plc
ISBN 1 85881 455 3

contents

lost ball
stops play

alan durant

We'd already thrashed them at our place. Twelve seven the score was, and it would have been thirteen if Chippy's trainer hadn't split and tripped him up with an open goal in front of him and not a Gordon Road Rover in sight. But would the Rovers accept their defeat? Would they shake hands like sportsmen and admit that the best team had won? That the Fairview Estate All Stars were the undisputed champions of Parkside and Gordon Road Rovers were rubbish? Would they heck.

'We can't play on concrete,' says Big Bennet. 'We play on grass. Anyway, concrete's not a proper football surface. Man United don't play on concrete, do they?'

'Man United play football,' sneers Kieron, or 'Incey' as we call him because he looks a bit like Paul Ince – well, from the back. Then Baby Bennet, Big Bennet's little brother, pipes up.

'We'd murder you at our place,' he says.

'You'd never,' says Natty. That's Natalie Peters, our striker.

'We would too,' Baby Bennet insists. And that's how come we're on Gordon Green this afternoon playing Gordon Road Rovers in a rematch.

It's a laugh, though, them calling this pitch grass. It's got more bald patches than Chippy's dad and the grass that's there is brown and straggly. The only proper grass is down the sides where it's so long you could lose the ball in it. There's a massive great tree on the pitch too, half away along one of the sides.

'Call this a pitch,' grumbles Jumping Jack Roberts, our goalie.

'You can concede the match if you like,' says Brian Drain, 'Braindrain', their goalie, who knows every football rule in the book and a few that haven't been written yet. He wants to be a referee when he grows up, and he's already been on a couple of courses. Unfortunately he's not on one this afternoon.

'We're not conceding nothing,' says Incey fiercely. I don't reckon he knows what Braindrain's on about but anyway he doesn't like his tone.

'We can thrash you on any surface,' says Natalie and, noisily, we all agree.

'Come on, then,' says Big Bennet. 'Let's get started.'

The match is five-a-side and this is how the two teams line up:

Fairview Estate All Stars (hurrah!)

'Jumping Jack' Roberts.

Sam Strong (me!)

Kieron 'Incey' Bishop.

Li 'Chippy' Ho.

Natty Peters.

Gordon Road Rovers (boo, hiss!)
Brain 'Braindrain' Drain
Harry 'Crazy Horse' McNeil
Ivan 'Hacker' Hughes
Big Bennet
Baby Bennet

The game goes like a dream. Chippy and Natty
both hit hat-tricks, Kieron gets a couple and I score
one direct from a free kick. With a minute left, we're
nine four up and the Rovers are nowhere. We're on
the rampage, looking for that one goal that'll see us
into double figures when Braindrain strikes. He gets
to a long punt from Jumping Jack just ahead of Natty
and grabs the ball. Then he waves his team upfield.
That's not the way he faces, though. He turns sort of
sideways towards the big tree. Then he swings his foot
and gives the ball an almighty boot. We all look up as
the ball soars into the sky like a rocket powered
marshmallow. Up and up it goes. And it doesn't come
down – not to the ground anyway. It drops a little and
nestles neatly among the branches of the tree – a long
way up.

We stand for a moment or two, totally gob-
smacked.

'What you do that for?' says Incey eventually.

'Lost ball stops play,' says Braindrain smugly.

'But you did that on purpose,' says Natty.

'I can kick the ball wherever I like,' says Braindrain.

'And I can kick you wherever I like an' all,' says Jumping Jack who's come marching all the way up the pitch with a face like Monday morning.

'We'll have to call it a draw,' says Big Bennet with a shrug.

'A draw!' I say. 'You've got to be joking. We were murdering you.'

'That's the rules,' says Braindrain. 'If the ball is lost, then the game can't go on. That means the result's a draw.'

'A draw!' wails Incey. 'Never.'

Things look like they're going to turn as ugly as one of Hacker Hughes's slide tackles when Chippy raises a hand and says, 'Hey, guys, who says the game finished?' I'm just about to ask him where his ears have been hiding for the last few minutes, when he goes on, 'I can climb the tree, no problem. I get the ball.' We look at Chippy, then we look at the tree. Chippy's about three foot from head to toe and the tree's roughly ten miles high. Big Bennet laughs.

'You can't climb that,' he says.

'Sure, I can climb,' says Chippy with a grin. 'I climb chestnuts all the time.'

'It's not a chestnut tree actually,' says Braindrain smugly. 'It's a sycamore.'

'I'm sick of it all right,' Jumping Jack moans.

'No, no. I can climb. You see,' says Chippy confidently.

Then he's off. And, boy, can he climb! I've never seen Chippy's mum but I'm starting to think that maybe she's a mountain goat the way Chippy shins up that tree. In no time at all, he's half way up and the Gordon Road lot are looking sick as parrots. We, of course, are over the moon.

'Whoa! Go it, Chippy!' we shout. This is much more exciting than the match.

However … like the match, Chippy's climb comes to a sad and sudden conclusion.

Chippy's almost up to where the ball is lying when the branch he's standing on snaps. Chippy slips and down he drops. Luckily, though, his fall is broken by some leafy branches below and when we call up anxiously to see if he's okay there's a rustle of leaves and a round, very pale face peeks down at us.

'No problem,' Chippy says, but he doesn't sound half as cheerful as he did before he started climbing. 'I come down now,' he says meekly. There'd be no point in him going up again anyway – or any of the rest of us for that matter; the ball's out of reach now that branch has snapped off. Having looked a bit worried for a minute or so when Chippy was plumetting, Big Bennet is all grinny again now.

'That's it then, eh?' he says.

'Yeah, let's go home,' pipes his baby brother. Everyone's looking at me 'cause I'm the captain, but I don't know what to say. No way do I want this game to end like this, no way. What can I do, though?

'I got an idea,' says Jumping Jack just as Chippy reappears back on earth again, looking as floppy as a fish in his Dad's shop before it goes in the fryer. 'Come on,' says Jumping Jack to us.

'How do we know you'll come back?' says Hacker Hughes suspiciously.

'Yes,' says Braindrain. 'If you all go, we can call off the match you know. It's in the rules.' I give him a look like in my opinion the name Drain is too good for him; he should be called Sewer.

'It's okay,' says Chippy bravely. 'I stay.' And so it's agreed.

'We're not waiting long, though,' Big Bennet calls, as we follow Jumping Jack across the green.

Jumping Jack's idea is this: his mum's got a long pole she uses to prop up her washing line; we borrow it and use it to get the ball out of the tree. Sounds simple enough. However, when we get to JJ's house and go out into the garden, we discover two big problems: one, the pole is at this moment holding up the entire Roberts family weekly wash and, two, I don't reckon it's nearly long enough anyway.

'Oi, Jack, are these yours?' says Incey with a grin, pointing at a pair of horrible flowery knickers.

'Of course they're not,' says JJ hotly. 'They're my sister's.'

'I don't care if they're your dog's,' I say. 'How are we supposed to get this pole? And anyway it's too short.'

'It's not,' says JJ. 'It extends, doesn't it?'

'Great,' I say. 'But it seems to be a bit busy just now.'

'It's all right,' says JJ, 'we'll take it. The washing's nearly dry anyway.'

'Are you sure?' says Natty, eyeing up a soaking wet towel.

'Yeah,' says JJ and he goes over to the pole and starts to pull at it. It's not easy to get it away from the line and when he finally manages it with a massive tug, he falls flat on his back.

'Ow!' he cries as the pole clunks him a good one, right on the forehead. But there's no time to worry about that. We're all too busy taking in the disaster scene that was Jack's mum's high-flying washing line: towels and sheets are trailing in the flower beds; the odd sock has decided to make a leap for freedom; a bra is draped over Incey's head like earflaps … And then there's this almighty, terrifying shriek.

'My washing! What's happened to my washing!' It's Jumping Jack's mum and she sounds like murder. We don't hang about. We turn and run.

'Great idea, Jack,' says Incey when we're safely out of murder distance. He's very image-conscious is Incey and it didn't do much for his image having a bra wrapped round his head.

'Well,' growls Jumping Jack, 'It wasn't my fault. There wasn't any washing on the line when I went out, was there?'

'Hmmm,' says Incey. There's a deafening silence for a few moments like there was one minute to go in the Cup Final and our team had just gone a goal down. Then Natty speaks.

'Hey, guys,' she says, 'don't worry. It's okay, I've got an idea …'

Natty's idea is this: her dad's a window-cleaner and he's got lots of ladders, including one that's about a mile long (so Natty says); so we borrow one to get our ball down from the tree.

'Great!' we say, our spirits rising, our faces all smiles again, like our team just got the equaliser to take the match into extra time. Then we race round to Natty's.

This time, we decide, we'll ask first before we walk off with any ladder. Natty goes in the house to find her dad. But there's no sign of him and her mum's gone to the gym. Leaning against the front of the house, though, is the longest ladder I have ever seen. It would do the job, easy. The only problem is getting it down without causing terminal damage to ourselves, Natty's house, Natty's dad's van, plus anything and anybody else that happens to be in the street. We've got to go for it, though. It's too good an opportunity to miss. So, very carefully, we start to drag the ladder back. It weighs a ton, but eventually we manage to move it a bit. It scrapes along then sort of hops over the gutter and crashes against the wall underneath so hard that Natty and Kieron both fall over. Then the trouble begins.

'Oi! Who's mucking about with my ladder!'

We hear the angry voice of Natty's dad a moment before we see his (equally angry) face glaring down at us. He looks like an ogre who's just had his golden-egg-laying hen nicked. 'You kids!' he roars. 'What do you think you're doing?'

By the time we've apologised, explained, grovelled, and helped get the ladder back up where it was, we've wasted several precious minutes. For all we know the Gordon Road lot could be bidding Chippy a fond farewell at this very moment, but we can't give up. And, anyway, Incey's got an idea.

Incey's idea is this: we go and get his big brother. Incey's big for his age – he's head and shoulders above the rest of us – but his big brother Lynton's a giant. He's the best highjumper and basketball player in his school – in all the schools in the area. In fact, Incey tells us as we make our way round his house, Lynton may well be the best highjumper and basketball player in any school in the whole country. If the walk was much longer, he'd probably be the best high-jumper and basketball player in the entire universe.

'If anyone can get that ball down, Lynton can,' Incey says with total confidence.

The problem is Lynton won't. He's in the bath and he doesn't want to be disturbed.

'I just had a hard workout down the track, guys,' he says. 'Now leave me be, will you.'

'Hey, Lynton!' Incey shouts at the locked bathroom door. 'You've got to come. If we don't get that ball down, the match is a draw.' The immediate response is a loud slushing sound as Lynton settles himself in for a long wallow.

'So it's a draw,' he says finally. 'What's the problem. You win some, you lose some, you draw some. That's life.' This is rich, I reckon, coming from the best highjumper and basketball player in the universe. I mean, when did he last lose or draw? There's no point in hanging around any longer, though: Lynton's not coming and that's that.

There's only one option left. I don't like it, I'd never

have suggested it. But, it's this or we don't get our win. And I want that win.

'We'll have to borrow Dan's ball,' I say grimly. Dan's my older brother. He's got a brilliant football he bought with his birthday money. He loves that ball; it's his favourite possession. He won't let me touch it. He won't even let me look at it. He's told me, several times, in great and gory detail, just what he'll do to me if he ever catches me so much as laying my little finger on it. He'd never lend it to me in a million years. Only, today he's gone fishing with Uncle Mike ...

Mum's in the kitchen when we come in at the backdoor.

'Hi, Sam,' she says.

'Hi, Mum,' I say. Then, casually, 'Is Dan back yet?' Then she clocks Kieron and JJ standing behind me (we sent Natty back to Gordon Green to tell them we were on our way with a new ball). 'What are you lot up to?' she asks suspiciously.

'Oh, nothing,' I say, trying to sound airy as the breeze. 'We're just going to look at some stuff in my bedroom.'

'Oh,' says Mum. 'Well I'm just off out the front to pick some herbs.'

'OK,' I say. We follow her along the hallway then quickly climb the stairs. After that it's a cinch. We're in and out of Dan's room faster than you can say 'Ryan Giggs'. Then we speed down the stairs and head for the kitchen door ... and that's when it all goes wrong – 'cause when I push the door open, who do I see sitting there but Uncle Mike and Dan. Luckily, Dan's got his back to me, but Uncle Mike's seen me so I can't go back. All I can do is pass the ball behind me and walk on in.

'Hi,' I say. 'You're back early. Had a good fish?'

'Terrific,' says Uncle Mike. 'Eh, Dan?'

'Yeah,' says Dan, not looking at me, grinning at Uncle Mike. 'I caught a seven pounder.'

'Wow! Great!' I say. 'A seven pounder! That's ... big.' As I speak this garbage, I'm sort of shuffling across the kitchen towards the back door, with the others following behind. We're all squashed together like Siamese triplets, trying to hide the ball, which I can feel pushing into my back and have worked out must be nestling under JJ's jumper. It nearly works too. Nearly. I'm just a foot from the door and freedom when Uncle Mike stops us in our tracks.

'You've put on a bit of weight there, Jack, haven't you?' he says.

'Oh, yeah,' says JJ shakily. 'Yeah. Been eating a lot of cakes and stuff.'

Uncle Mike grins. 'It looks like you've swallowed a football,' he says and Dan laughs. I laugh too, a small forced laugh and so does Incey. JJ smiles sort of sheepishly as if he's just let in a soft goal. Then Dan stops laughing. His face clouds over like he's just found out his seven pounder was actually a large boot.

'If that's my football you've got there ...' he growls. And that's that. The game's up. Over. The final whistle's been blown. We've lost.

We troop back to Gordon Green a defeated side. We've only been gone twenty minutes but it seems like a lifetime. All our efforts have been for nothing. And, as if this wasn't bad enough, a big wind's got up and is trying to blow our heads off.

'There'll be another day,' Incey shouts over the wind. But that's no consolation. We want to beat those Gordon goons today.

'So you got here at last,' Big Bennet greets us. 'You think we've got nothing better to do than hang around in this wind waiting for you.'

'It was your goalie that kicked the ball in the tree remember,' says Jumping Jack grumpily.

'Yeah, well,' says Big Bennet. 'You got the ball or what?'

I glare at him. 'No,' I say eventually. 'We haven't.'

Big Bennet's face looks as happy as Christmas. 'That's it then,' he says. 'Game's over. It's a draw.'

'A draw,' Braindrain repeats, as if we needed to hear it a second time.

'We want a rematch,' says Kieron.

'Yeah, yeah,' says Big Bennet. 'We'll …'

We don't hear what they're going to do, though, because Big Bennet's words get lost in a roaring rush of wind that's so strong it nearly lifts Baby Bennet right off his feet.

It does something else too.

There's a heavy thud behind us and we all jump. Then we turn to see what's fallen … It's the ball. The wind's brought down the ball! Half of us look at it like it's the winning lottery ticket, the other half like it's a bowl of cabbage stew. I don't have to tell you which is which.

'Right, then,' I say. 'Let's finish the match …'

The last minute is a massacre. Chippy, Natty and Incey each rattle in another goal just like that and the final score is 12–4. Not even Braindrain can find a way of wriggling out of this one. The Gordon Road Rovers have been beaten fair and square. Fairview Estate All Stars are the undisputed champions of Parkside!

'You know,' says Incey, as we stroll home in triumph, 'maybe we should play on grass all the time.' He grins. 'After all, Man United don't play on concrete, do they?'

the happy team

alan gibbons

We've always been a happy team. We had to be when you think about it. It's the names, you see. There's me for a start, Danny Merrie. Then there's my best mate, Mark Jolley. You think that's a bit of a coincidence? You ain't heard nothing yet. Our captain's the same. Pete Smiley, he's called. That's wily Smiley to his mates, on account of his grasp of soccer tactics.

My dad says it must be something in the water. How else would you get a Merrie, a Jolley and a Smiley in one school, never mind in one team?

Mum say maybe it's the history of our area. It probably goes back to the Middle Ages or something. You know, like men in brown nightgowns and bald heads. Or plague pits. Yes, maybe our great-great-great-great grandparents were medieval comedians. Or, more likely still, village idiots!

Personally, I think it's all one big coincidence. Like the charity football competition. We couldn't believe it when the letter came round school. A local company was donating a cash prize to support junior sports. It was the answer to our prayers. It's Guppy, you see. His little sister was really ill. She was born ill, some tube inside her didn't work properly. And I don't mean sick-on-your-sheets ill, or kiss-it-better ill.

No, Ramila was in a bad way. Let's be honest, she was dying. We all felt sorry for Guppy. He was great, always cheerful and full of jokes. A proper Happy Team member. He adored Ramila. We thought he was weird sometimes. Most of us can't stand our little brothers and sisters. Well, who wants something round the house that's wet at both ends, screams a lot and gets all the attention? But Guppy was proud of his sister. She was brave. Brave the way a football is round.

So the moment I saw the charity soccer competition letter pinned up outside the head's office I went looking for Guppy.

'Seen this?' I asked.

Guppy took the letter and just stared at me. For a moment I thought he was going to cry. But he didn't. That would be too naff by half. His voice went really low.

'For Ramila, you mean?'

'Of course for Ramila,' I told him. 'Five hundred pounds to the winning team, it says. To be paid to a charity of their choice. Well, I can't think of a better cause than a dying kid, can you?'

'No.'

Guppy was excited. His family's been raising money for months. Ramila's only got one chance. There's this operation, but they don't do it in Britain. She'll have to go to America and it will cost a fortune.

The people round our way have been amazing. All the shops have got posters with Ramila's face on them, and collecting tins. The black cabs are the same. They've got them up too. You get the odd idiot who scribbles things on the posters. You know, 'Paki' and rubbish like that, but most people are great. A sick kid's a sick kid in any language and that's all that matters. With the five hundred pounds prize money we would reach the target.

'Let's tell the lads,' said Guppy.

So we did.

They jumped at it, of course. That's the sort of team we are. All for one and one for all. Like I told you, happy. Well, except for Slammer. With him, it's more a case of all for me. On the quiet, I think he's the one who scribbled on Ramila's posters, but I'd decided not to let on to Guppy. Slammer's never fitted in properly. It's not that he can't play. No, he's a natural striker and he's got a good engine. Our manager, Tommy Dolan, thinks Slammer could even get a trial for Everton or Liverpool. But it's his personality that's wrong. He had a big fight with Guppy once. He wouldn't stop skitting him. That's why I didn't tell Guppy about the posters. Bad for team morale.

You could say Slammer finds it difficult to be a team player, and I'm putting it politely.

'Sounds stupid to me,' said Slammer, the moment we'd finished.

'Why's it stupid?' asked Mark.

'Well, why can't we keep the money ourselves?'

'Because it's to help other people, that's why,' said Mark.

Slammer frowned. There was only one sort of people he wanted to help – and that was himself.

Mark shook his head. He doesn't like Slammer, but then who does? If he wasn't our best player, he would have had the old heave-ho months ago.

'The whole thing's a waste of time, if you ask me,' said Slammer.

'Nobody *was* asking you,' Mark snapped.

Slammer just sulked, but then he always does, and while he sulked we made plans. After a bit of argy bargy the plans became one Master Plan, and it went something like this:

One Post off the application form. (That was the easy bit).

Two Hammer the opposition.

Three Hand the cheque over to Guppy's mum and dad.

Four Wave Ramila off at the airport.

Not much of a Master Plan, you might think, but it suited us fine. All except Slammer. Just when we were all smiles (well, we are the Happy Team) he piped up, grumbling as usual.

'How come the money has to go to *his* family?' he demanded, nodding in Guppy's direction.

'Because,' Mark told him shortly, 'Guppy's the one with the sick sister.'

'Well, I don't think it's fair,' snorted Slammer.

'Look,' I said, noticing steam starting to come out of Mark's ears. 'Make your mind up, Slammer. Are you in or out?'

Slammer gave Guppy a sidelong glance. 'In,' he said after a long pause.

Somehow none of us liked the way he said it. A sly sort of grin came across his face. It was like he'd suddenly come up with his own Master Plan.

'What's with him?' asked Mark.

'Beats me,' I answered. 'Nothing to bother us, anyway.'

But I was wrong. Dead wrong, as we were soon to find out.

It was a fortnight before we got a reply to our application, but it was worth the wait.

'We're in!' Pete announced. 'Qualifying match this Saturday, then a knockout tournament the following week if we get through.'

'*If* we get through!' scoffed Mark. 'We'll walk it.'

He had good cause to be confident. We were running away with the North Liverpool Junior League. Our manager, Tommy Dolan, said we were unstoppable. On the back of five straight wins, we were leading the league by six clear points.

'A cup competition's a bit different, of course,' said Guppy.

'Yeah,' said Mark. 'We play the league for fun. This,' he waved the letter, 'this is for a mate.'

Everybody started digging Guppy in the ribs and messing his hair. He looked embarrassed. But happy.

That's when I noticed Slammer out of the corner of my eye. He was staring. Just staring at Guppy. Like he was his worst enemy. Right away I was thinking about how Slammer had grinned, and the way we all thought he'd written on the posters and I found myself wondering if Mark wasn't getting just a bit too confident.

As it turned out, I was worrying over nothing. When Saturday came round, we were up against this outfit called Croxteth Celtic. It wasn't easy, but we kept our nerve. They flew at us right from the kick-off. Mad, they were.

We'd already had a couple of scares when they got a free kick on the edge of the box. Well, this lanky kid lollops up and hits a screamer of a free kick. Mark was in the wall and it was going straight at him until he ducked. It cannoned off the bar with a tremendous crack.

'You ducked,' screamed Pete. 'There's no point in being part of the wall if you get out of the way of the ball. What did you duck for?'

'If I hadn't,' Mark retorted irritably, 'it would have taken my rotten head off.'

That was the last time they had us rattled though, the team *and* the crossbar. Celtic tired after that and we eventually ran out 4–1 winners. Guppy and Pete scored, but Slammer was our man of the match again. He scored two and made both the others. No wonder he walked off smiling. The trouble is, I couldn't help wondering if he didn't have something else on his mind beside his brace of goals. Mark and Pete reckoned I was worrying about nothing, but I wasn't so sure. If you'd seen the way Slammer was grinning, you'd know what I mean. We're talking crocodiles.

'Three more wins,' said Mark on the way home, and Ramila's off to the States.'

'And the way Slammer's playing,' Pete chimed in, 'we're a dead cert.'

Though I didn't let on, this funny idea kept rattling round in my brain. What if Slammer stopped playing?

By the following Saturday, I'd almost forgotten about my suspicions. It was the excitement, I suppose. For a start, Guppy's dad had been in touch with the hospital in America. They could do the operation within a month. They just needed the money.

'Do you think we can do it?' asked Guppy as we got changed.

'Think?' said Mark. 'I *know*.'

'Tell you what,' said Pete, glancing at the changing-room clock. 'Old Slammer's cutting it fine.' 'Yes,' said Guppy. 'He is, isn't he?'

Cutting it fine was an understatement. As we clattered out of the changing-room we looked up and down the road. No Slammer. As we jogged onto the pitch we gave a last look round. Still no Slammer.

'You'd think he could have phoned,' Pete complained. 'He's only our star player.'

'Forget it,' said Mark. 'Tell Gerry Jones to get his tackle off. We'll have to use our sub. Slammer or no Slammer, we're going to win this.'

A couple of words went unspoken. For Ramila. But Mark would never have said anything that soppy.

I glanced at the other quarter-finals taking place on the other pitches. So this was Slammer's plan. Stay away and hope we lose. Somehow, I felt relieved. I'd expected a lot worse from him.

Slammer's absence didn't make much difference in the first match. We hammered our opponents 6–3. The semi-final was tougher though. We had to come back from behind twice and at full time it was all square, 2–2.

'Penalty shootout,' grumbled Tommy Dolan. 'And we're lucky to be in that. We're missing Slammer.'

But not when it came to penalties. We converted every one. The only trouble is, so did the other side.

'Miss it,' whispered Guppy as their fourth penalty-taker placed the ball.

I smiled. It wasn't like Guppy to wish ill on anyone, but I suppose this was an exception.

'Please miss it,' Guppy whispered.

The lad did too. By a mile.

'You certainly put the mockers on him,' said Pete.

'Yes,' said Guppy with a smile. 'I did, didn't I?'

He glanced at his mum and dad standing on the touch-line with Ramila. It looked like the dream was coming true.

Mark slotted home his penalty. Another miss by the opposition and we were home and dry.

'Got the evil eye ready, Guppy?' I asked.

Guppy smiled. Quietly. But when the penalty-taker spooned it over the bar he roared. Loudly.

'That's it,' said Pete. 'We're in the final. Come on, the other semi is still playing. Let's see who we're up against.'

As we walked across the playing field we were smiling from ear to ear. That's when we spotted him.

'Slammer!'

The smiles vanished.

'Where?'

'There.'

'The traitor,' said Mark, clenching his fists. 'The rotten traitor. Who's that he's playing for?'

'Stoneycroft Rovers,' Tommy Dolan told us. 'I've been watching them. They're a useful outfit.'

Useful was right. Just before the final whistle Slammer stuck a cracking volley. It was the winner. 4–3.

As Slammer came off, Pete had a go at him. 'This is a dirty trick. You know how much this means to Guppy.'

Slammer gave a low, throaty chuckle. 'Yes. Why do you think I did it? You're going to get buried.'

'That's it, then,' groaned Guppy. 'We've had it.'

'No we haven't,' said Pete.

'But he was our best player. Now they've got him.'

'So we reorganise,' said Pete. 'Somebody's got to mark him out of the game.'

'That means me,' said Mark. 'Get it? Mark the marker.'

But come the final, Mark the marker was Mark the muffer. We were two-nil down in ten minutes. Slammer made one and scored one. The dream was fading fast.

'Enjoying the match?' gloated Slammer as he jogged past.

We just turned away.

'We're getting roasted,' Pete complained as he retrieved the ball from our net. 'And it's all down to Slammer.'

I saw him looking at us. I saw the grin.

'Maybe Mark's the wrong person to put on Slammer,' I murmured.

'So who?'

'Somebody with more reason to stop him,' I said. 'Guppy.'

'Guppy?' said Pete. 'But tackling's not his game.'

'It is now,' I told him.

'Meaning?'

'Meaning. I know who scribbled on the posters.'

Guppy looked across the pitch. 'You mean?'

'Yeah, Slammer.'

From the re-start Stoneycroft came at us again. Slammer picked up the ball in the channels and surged forward. But it had become a grudge match. Guppy was tackling like a Rottweiler.

'Nice one,' said Mark.

A minute later Slammer had it again. But Guppy got in his tackle. Like a Pit Bull. We watched Slammer rising gingerly to his feet. The grin had vanished.

Next time Slammer got the ball he just pushed it away. Before Guppy could even tackle.

'Now we can make a game of it,' said Pete.

Mark was happier in attack than man-to-man marking. He picked the ball up on the left and drove into the box. Determined to make up for losing out in the duel with Guppy, Slammer came in hard.

'Penalty!'

Mark placed the ball. With a short run-up he side-footed it to the goalie's left. 2–1.

Tommy Dolan was on the touch-line, holding up five fingers. As we laid siege to their area, Stoneycroft brought every man back. Twice, we had shots scrambled off the line. I glanced at the touch-line. Tommy Dolan was gesturing. Three fingers. Three minutes.

Guppy had the ball on the edge of the area, jinking and dribbling.

'Square,' shouted Pete suddenly. 'Across the box.'

Guppy didn't even look up. He just back-heeled it. Pete stuck it hard and low. I knew it was coming my way so I stuck out a foot. It could have gone anywhere. But it deflected into the net. 2–2.

Suddenly Slammer was sweating. And not because of the running he was doing. His side was rocking on its heels. In less than thirty seconds we were pinning them back in their own half again. Pete hit the post and I had a shot palmed over the bar. I glanced at Tommy Dolan. He was drawing his index finger across his throat. The ref was going to blow any moment.

'I don't fancy another penalty shoot-out,' said Pete. 'Everybody up for the corner.'

As it came over I leapt, but it was too high. I was dropping back to the ground when I saw somebody coming in on my left. Guppy. He got right over the ball and headed it down. 3–2.

The ref didn't even get to blow the whistle. We'd won. I didn't even see Slammer after that. But I knew for certain the grin was gone for good. There isn't much more to tell, really. Ramila had the operation and she's well on the mend. So much so that Guppy's even started saying what a pain she is! As for the team, we went on to win the league.

Now that's what I call a happy team!

goalkeeping? easy!

michael hardcastle

Andy Bourne was bouncing the ball on the goal-line and then throwing it to team-mates who tried to beat him with a header.

'Easiest job in the world, that,' scoffed Travis Jarman after seeing Andy catch his close-range shot. 'Anybody can do it.'

'Rubbish!' Andy fired back at him. 'A goalie's got to be really talented in all sorts of ways that you'd never even think of. All you do is stick the ball in the net when you get the chance. *And* you've got other strikers to help you. I'm always on my own, the very last line of defence. You'd get bored on your own, Trav. You'd lose concentration.'

'No I wouldn't! Listen, I played in goal loads of times before I became a top striker. So I know I'm good.'

'That's enough, you two,' said George Banner, captain of Faxenby Flyers, their team. 'We're supposed to be practising our skills for the game against Colombard, not arguing with each other. Whatever happened to our team spirit?'

Moments before the Colombard match was due to kick off Andy Bourne was missing.

'You know, I think it's deliberate,' said Jonathan.

'He wants Travis to prove his boasts about being a good goalie.'

'Oh, I don't think so,' said George. 'Andy's too loyal to let us down like that. He loves keeping goal, so he wouldn't miss a game unless he was ill or injured. I'll get one of the parents over there to ring him.' He turned to Travis. 'Trav, we need a goalie now, so how about it? I mean, I can get Gary, the sub, to take your place up front. He'd be useless in goal. Too small, to start with.'

'Yeah, sure, be glad to star between the posts,' Travis said enthusiastically, much to George's surprise. 'Andy will never get his place back after my performance.'

'Just don't let us down, that's all,' warned George. 'Colombard are not a bad side. Decent defenders, anyway.'

'Well, if you need goals from me I'll switch back to striker easily,' Travis offered.

'No way!' said George firmly. 'You're our goalie now, so your job is to prevent goals, not score 'em!'

News that Faxenby were playing an inexperienced goalkeeper soon spread. Colombard began to hit shots from every range but Travis dealt confidently with all of them. Yelling encouragement to his fellow defenders, he pointed out that they could pass the ball back to him whenever they liked. Up front, Faxenby were not playing well against a tall, steady defence. Gary could never win the ball in the air and he fluffed a couple of easy chances in the box.

'I'd've put those away before their goalie could even blink,' claimed Travis, dancing up and down with annoyance. His team-mates didn't doubt that but knew he had to stay where he was.

Suddenly, a Colombard striker broke through with the ball at his feet and only one defender and Travis to beat. The defender chased after him, launched a sliding tackle and brought him crashing to the ground. It had to be a penalty. Travis tried to protest but the ref wouldn't listen. Now, Travis knew, he would be tested to the full.

Colombard's stocky captain strode up, put the ball on the spot and fired it powerfully towards the roof of the net. Travis hadn't moved a millimetre before the ball was kicked, so when it flew almost straight at him all he had to do was jump and, with one hand, tip it over the bar. He'd saved his first penalty! As the team gathered in the box for the corner kick most said 'Great save!' and patted him on the back. Travis looked smug. After all, he hadn't expected to be beaten. What's more, he nonchalantly jumped out to take the ball from the corner kick and punt it up-field. Life for a goalie, he was deciding, was far easier than life for a striker.

A few minutes later he was changing his mind.

Jonathan, attempting a clearance in a crowded goal-mouth, miskicked completely. The ball sliced upwards and then the spin turned it towards the net. Although taken by surprise, Travis leapt sideways and almost managed to get a hand to it. But it was impossible to prevent it dropping just inside the post for a calamitous own goal.

'You maniac!' Travis yelled at the culprit.

'Sorry, sorry, sorry!' apologised Jonathan, his face as scarlet as his Faxenby shirt.

'Better go down on your knees to George, he'll never forgive you,' said Dale, a fellow defender.

George, however, soon had something to celebrate. For, as if to match Faxenby in style, Colombard also conceded an own goal in bizarre circumstances.

Gary, desperate to keep his place as a striker, charged in from the left wing and fired the ball furiously into the box in the hope that someone would get to it. The only player who did was the Colombard sweeper. Confident he knew where his goalkeeper was, he trapped the ball and in the same movement turned it sideways for his keeper to clear. But the goalie had moved in another direction and he watched helplessly as the ball trickled over the goal-line. Gary wanted to claim it but George wouldn't allow that.

'Just be thankful we're on level terms,' he said. 'We haven't played well enough to get a point.'

That was how the match ended. In the dressing-room Travis asked about Andy Bourne.

'Damaged his ankle, falling off something, according to his mum when Mr Peel rang her,' George reported. 'Don't know if he'll be fit for the Beldock game but you seemed to manage okay. Better than I expected, actually.'

'*Told* you I was good,' Trav responded, irritated that his captain hadn't believed him or praised him sufficiently. 'But I'd've scored a hatful today if I'd been up-front. Gary should shoot himself for missing so many.'

When he set out to visit Andy that evening Travis still wasn't sure whether he really wanted to continue keeping goal, but after all he'd said to Andy and George he knew he couldn't admit that publicly. So much would depend on Andy's health.

Things definitely didn't look good when Mrs Bourne ushered him into the sitting-room. For Andy was reclining on the sofa, his legs bare and his right ankle not only heavily strapped but also packed in ice.

'You haven't moved, have you?' his mother demanded sharply. 'How can I?' enquired Andy. He glanced at Travis and seemed as embarrassed as Jonathan was at scoring an own goal.

'You haven't broken it, have you?' Travis asked

anxiously, handing over some chocolate he'd brought to share with his injured team-mate. Andy shook his head.

'Just sprained the ligaments or something like that. The ice is getting the swelling down. Wish I hadn't done it. The pain was terrible.'

'So how'd you do it?' Travis wanted to know.

'Swinging from a swing,' said Andy. 'I mean, there wasn't a seat in it, just a frame. I was moving on it like –'

'– like a monkey?' laughed Travis.

'Like a monkey, indeed,' agreed Mrs Bourne, coming in at that moment. 'He does it from door frames, too, and it's got to stop. His arms are quite long enough, thank you. No more, Andrew, or it'll be the end of football for you *for ever*!'

'I do it to *strengthen* my arms, not just lengthen them,' he protested, but his mother, after cuffing a cushion or two, had gone again. He looked at Travis for understanding and Travis, a believer in total fitness himself, nodded. 'I mean, I want to go right to the top as a goalie, so I've got to be brilliant. *Now*. I just wish our defence didn't keep letting me down by giving away stupid goals. Players like Dale make me really mad. He doesn't listen to what I tell him and he doesn't talk to the rest of the defence when he should do. You know, *warn* them what's happening. People can't see out of the back of their heads, can they?'

'Yeah, I know just what you mean,' Travis said. 'Same thing happened today with Jonathan. Took his eye off the ball and sliced it into our own net. Crazy! Gave me no chance of a save and cost us three points. Well, two, because we did get a draw. Made me so mad!'

'But you wouldn't get blamed for that, Trav, because you're not the real goalkeeper. If I do the slightest thing wrong, though, I get all the blame. Goalies are always a soft target for abuse, I can tell you. Our mistakes are never forgiven.'

Travis nodded again. He was thinking about the praise that goalies sometimes got for making out-of-this-world saves; somehow that didn't compare with the adulation heaped on the scorer of a winning goal in a Cup-tie or a top-of-the-table clash.

'When do you think you'll be back in action, Andy?' he asked.

'No idea,' said Andy gloomily. 'The doc says I've got to rest up my ankle for a bit before I try to run. And Mum is threatening to keep me off football for good because she says it's dangerous. She's said that before and usually I get her to change her mind. *Usually*. But she thinks this is a dire injury.'

'So I expect I'll be in goal for the Beldock game, then,' said Travis.

'Bound to be. But you said you like it!' Andy pointed out. 'And you didn't let in a goal, did you?

Well, not a real one. With me on the injured list George needs you.'

After a brief discussion about the prospects for the match against one of the League's toughest teams Travis left. At home he watched a video of one of his heroes in action and thought about his own future.

'You okay?' his mum asked him. 'Never known you so quiet.'

'Got a lot on my mind,' Travis confessed.

'Well, if it's about football, stop worrying,' said his mum. 'Everybody says you're very good at what you do – or so I'm told.'

'Right,' said Travis. 'But *what* do I do?' He didn't expect an answer and he didn't get one.

Beldock Bees were known, predictably, as the Stingers and they enjoyed their reputation of being an all-action side with a fondness for the counter-attack. If they went a goal down their supporters expected them to hit back immediately; and invariably they did, no matter how well their opponents defended.

'Our plan must be to attack *them* continously,' said George before the kick-off. 'That way we'll also be protecting our keeper and –'

'I don't *need* protecting!' Travis interrupted indignantly. 'I can take care of myself. Nobody'll get the ball past me, not even one of *our* defenders.' He couldn't help shooting a glance at Jonathan but

Jonathan just shrugged. He knew he didn't make a habit of scoring own goals.

Travis was wearing a new black sweater so that the colour didn't clash with the yellow of their opponents' shirts and the scarlet of Faxenby. He felt it made him stand out against everyone else and that, somehow, increased his confidence.

In the opening minutes of the match, however, he wished he was at the other end of the pitch. That was where the action was. Faxenby were faithfully following George's orders to attack and they swarmed around the Bees' goalmouth. Two or three times it seemed they must score but chances were missed through over-eagerness until at last Gary forced the ball over the line in a desperate scramble for possession. He was ecstatic. It was his first goal for the Flyers, and it was the happiest moment of his life. Travis signalled his congratulations but he knew he himself would have scored long before this if he'd been leading the attack.

Of course, Beldock tried to hit back immediately, only to find that the Faxenby midfield still had a firm grip and were letting nothing escape them. Then the Bees changed their tactics and began to hit long balls for their twin strikers to chase.

Dale and Jonathan and the rest of the defence were soon under real pressure. But they were coping well and Travis hadn't had a single shot to save until the

Bees' nippy, redhaired striker suddenly broke clear with only the goalkeeper to beat. Travis didn't hesitate. He dashed out, prepared to dive at the attacker's feet for the ball. As Travis went down the Beldock player tried to swerve round him, only to stumble. Then, in his eagerness to recover the ball which Travis managed to grab with one hand, he stepped on Travis's arm and then fell. In his rage and pain Travis hurled the ball at him as his opponent was getting to his feet. Promptly, the boy went down again.

'You really deserve a red card for that but I hate to send a schoolboy off!' snapped the referee. 'If you display the same violence again I shan't hesitate to dismiss you, so be warned.'

Travis took his time receiving treatment from the parent acting as the team's physio, because he knew the penalty couldn't be taken until he was ready to face the kick. The delay, he hoped, might put the kicker off. Unhappily for Faxenby, it didn't. This time Travis was given no chance to make a save as the ball whistled into the corner of the net. The Stingers had stung: the teams were level again. Travis nursed his arm and cursed his luck. None of his team-mates said 'Bad luck!' to him or anything like that. Plainly, they felt he was to blame for Beldock's goal. George, especially, looked really upset.

After that success, the Stingers kept up the momentum of their attacks, determined to take the lead. Travis was too busy to think about the pain in his arm. In any case, it didn't hinder his handling of the ball. An attacker who tried to bundle him over as a corner-kick was taken was fiercely rebuked by Travis.

'You've got a mouth as big as a goalmouth!' his opponent jeered. Travis felt like hitting him. He didn't know that the boy used the same phrase to wind up every goalie he met; he had a theory that the insult would infuriate them and they'd lose concentration and make mistakes. Sometimes it worked. But this time Travis's skills were not undermined and he remained in command of his net.

At half-time, however, George had a word with him.

'Look, whatever you do, stay cool. Don't get another card. We can't afford to have our goalie sent off. We'd have no chance against this lot with only ten men. There's nobody else I could trust between the posts.'

Travis nodded, pleased with the compliment but wishing it had been warmer. He remembered Andy's view of the treatment goalkeepers usually received from team-mates and spectators.

'Don't worry, skipper, I'll keep my temper and I'll keep a clean sheet from now on. I mean, they won't get another penalty, will they?'

But they did. Well into the second half Dale was involved in a tussle for the ball with an attacker on the edge of the box. The striker turned this way and that, trying to outwit Dale, but Dale stuck with him and then, stretching his foot out for the ball, pushed his opponent over. The ref blew and pointed to the spot, a harsh decision by any standards.

'Oh no, Ref, it can't be!' Travis protested. But then he had the sense to fall silent when the ref glared at him. Travis now had to work out where the kicker would hit his shot. He was the boy fouled by Dale, not the one who'd taken the previous kick.

The kicker ran in, let fly – and Travis completely lost sight of the ball. Instead, he grabbed at the object sailing towards him – and found himself holding a boot! The cheers of the Beldock spectators told him the ball had landed in the net but the astonishment on the face of the kicker matched Travis's.

'But it's a goal, isn't it?' the boy asked anxiously. 'I mean, my boot must have come loose when I was fouled.'

'Can't be a goal, I never saw the ball and I was hit by this stupid boot!' Travis hurled it to the ground where it was gratefully seized by the owner. The ref was talking things over with a linesman and they concluded no rule had been broken: the goal stood.

'Honestly, goalies have to cope with idiots!' Travis raged. 'If I'd been taking a penalty I'd've made sure my boots were properly fastened on. Honestly, it should never have been a goal ...'

Nobody was listening because the game had resumed and the Stingers were going all out for a third goal to clinch victory. There looked to be no hope of Faxenby getting the equaliser. Then, during a brief stoppage, George dashed over to Travis, tugging at his left ear, always a sign he'd made a decision.

'Let's have your jersey because I want you up front again,' he ordered. 'Can't risk having you sent off and I can see you're in the mood for a row. I'll take over. So you go and get us a goal, Trav.'

Travis thought of arguing and then changed his mind. Silently he handed over his black jersey and slipped on George's red shirt. After all, he knew he was getting what he really wanted. 'Good luck, skipper,' he said, and ran to join up with the attack in place of Gary who'd dropped back to fill George's place in midfield.

Full of energy, Travis ran at the opposition whenever he could get hold of the ball. He yelled for it, demanded it, pleaded for it. Beldock were awed by his pace and determination and their defence fell back, deeper and deeper. With five minutes of the match left, he made a goal for Gary who'd rushed forward to join in the hunt for the equaliser. And Gary took his chance neatly, slipping the ball past two defenders and then toe-poking it into the net.

Travis wasn't finished. He wanted victory. In the final minute, with the Bees helpless to stop him, Faxenby's top striker skipped over two desperate lunging tackles, slid the ball sideways to Gary and then screamed for its return. Gary obeyed. And Travis, swerving to his left and then to his right, lashed the ball beyond the goalkeeper's reach into the top of the net.

The match-winner disappeared under the piling bodies of his team-mates. It was, he knew, one of the best goals he'd ever scored. It was all he ever wanted to do.

'Nothing in the world is as good, as *glorious*, as getting a goal like that,' he told George when at last he could get to his feet. 'So you'd better make sure Andy's back between the posts for our next game. I'm staying up front.'

'Agreed,' grinned George, tugging at his left ear.

ugly me

alan brown

'm so ugly birds fall out of the sky when I look up at 'em. Milk turns sour on doorsteps as I go by. When I'm keeper the other football team can't score a goal. They see me and their shots go wide. It's all because I'm so ugly.

'You must be the ugliest person in the world,' says my mate Rich. I don't care, but I punch him anyway. Me and Rich, we're fighting friends. Sometimes I win and sometimes he wins. We don't hurt each other, much. That's what fighting friends are for.

Rich's got a twin sister called Abby. I never fight with Abby. She's beautiful, like a princess. When she's there all my words come out wrong, as if my tongue's too big for my mouth. I get clumsy, and drop things. I don't drop a thing when I'm in goal. Sticky Fingers, they call me.

'Hey, Sticky, we playing tonight?'

That was Tom. He's in my team. We don't have captains or anything – they just do what I say.

I can't sit still when we've got a game after school. Today I tried to make the teacher's writing fall off the blackboard by staring at it ever so hard. The words didn't fall off, but they did get a bit fuzzy. I felt Abby looking at me so I hid behind my desk lid.

On the way to the rec I started a traffic jam with

ugly-vision. I made all the cars conk out. You can do that sort of thing when you're as ugly as me, and nobody ever knows it was you. It doesn't work on buses and lorries. That's 'cos they're diesels.

We had to wait for Rich because he'd got the ball. Danny and me had a fight, just to pass the time. I was doing all right until he punched me on the nose. It made my eyes water and the other kids thought I was crying, but I wasn't.

My nose felt like it was broken, but Danny got me to wobble it from side to side and said it was all right. He wouldn't have wobbled his nose from side to side when it felt like it was broken.

When I could see again Rich was there. With the ball – and Abby.

'Woo boo doin 'ere?' I couldn't talk too good, at first.

'I want to play,' she said.

I looked round the team. They all looked the other way. I looked at Rich. He shrugged and started digging holes in the pitch with his toe.

I got my voice back. 'You want to play?' was all I could say.

Abby laughed. 'There's no need to cry about it,' she said.

'I'm not crying!' I yelled. She was making me all hot and confused again.

'I want to play,' she repeated.

'Why?'

'Why not?'

'That's not a good answer.'

'It wasn't a good question.'

Rich and Danny started to kick the ball about. Tom joined in.

'We don't have girls in our team,' I said. The ball came to a rest at Abby's feet. 'They're not good enough.'

Abby spun the ball backwards, flicked it up and juggled it on her feet and knees. Then she trapped it, dribbled round me faster than I could turn and lobbed it over my head to Rich. He grinned.

Abby ran off to join in the game. I needed to fight somebody, but there wasn't anybody left.

Danny picked one team and I picked the other. I wanted Rich on my side so I had to choose Abby as well. I thought that Danny would pick her first, but he chose all his friends like he always does.

By half-time we were four nil up. Abby scored three and Rich got one. I was bored. Nobody made me dive, and a goalie's not tested unless they have to dive. That's what I like best.

Danny groaned. 'Hey, Sticky. Have mercy. Give us a player to even things up a bit.'

'Who do you want?' I asked. We both knew who was the best player. I wanted to see whether he would ask for her.

Danny hesitated and Abby spoke for herself.

'I'll swop,' she said, going over to the other side. She had a look in her eye that said 'Look out!'

I got all the diving I wanted, and more.

Abby got one past me, and then two. She did banana shots, volleys and diving headers. By the time she got her third I was so tired that even Danny put one in our net.

With five minutes to go we were even at four all. Then Rich scrambled another and put us ahead again.

The shots came at me from all directions. I dived this way and that. I was half kicked to death. My sticky fingers kept snagging the ball, but I was slowing down.

I booted the ball up field to get a breather. When it came back I was still panting. Abby beat my defenders. Her foot went back for the shot. It was me against her.

Abby's foot came forward and I dived to cover the near post. Her shot went like a bullet towards the other side of the goal. I lay in the mud and watched helplessly. The ball sped over the crossbar!

'The ref must be a friend of yours!' Danny shouted.

Tom was blowing the whistle. We'd won five four!

Danny ranted and raved. I laughed. So did Abby.

I felt really good as I walked home. Just one thing bothered me. Why had Abby laughed? Surely she wanted to win?

The next day at school the game was big news. Danny was still moaning, but everyone else had enjoyed it.

'Hello, Sticky.'

I nodded, dumb again.

'You're a good keeper,' she said.

'You're a great player, Abby,' I croaked.

'Where're you sitting?'

Did I say that, or was it her? I was getting flustered again. Danny and his cronies started poking fun, so I had to sort them out. Boys in our class don't talk to girls.

By the time Mr Hawkins arrived I was back in my seat next to Simon Bates. Abby sat on her own. She smiled at me and I smiled back, rubbing my knuckles. What a nice day.

'When did Abby start sitting on her own, Rich?'

Rich laughed at me. I didn't hit him straight away, seeing he's Abby's brother. 'She used to sit with Nazzam who went home to Pakistan,' he said. 'Why?'

'Nothing.'

Rich laughed again. 'That's what Abby said. She was asking about you.'

We had a good fight.

The next day I went over to Abby's desk.

'Could I sit here for a bit? I'm not sitting with Simon any more.'

'Have you been fighting?' she asked.

'No, not exactly.'

'I don't want you here if you're fighting all the time.'

My pride wouldn't let me go back to Simon. 'All right,' I said.

Abby smiled and the sun shone. 'I'd like that then,' she said.

Mr Hawkins said it was all right to sit with Abby, but it was going to be hard to keep my promise not to fight. Boys in our class don't sit next to girls.

'Who's Prince Charming?' Danny taunted. He's so dumb I don't even mind.

'Prince Charming.'

It was like an echo. I glared round to see who it was -- Simon. So he was palling up with Danny. I rubbed my knuckles and they put their desk lids up and giggled.

They kept it up all day. It was more fun than lessons. Trilling 'Prince Charming, Prince Charming' like demented budgies.

I gave them ugly looks. They should have been terrified. They just laughed.

'Don't take any notice, Sticky,' said Abby.

Don't take any notice! It wasn't her they were laughing at. I used ugly-vision to make their hearts conk out. It didn't work. They must be diesels.

Next day I was early at school. Abby was late. It was just as well. Somebody had written 'Sticky loves Abby' on the board in the middle of a big red heart.

I knew who. Simon rubbed it off. Danny was a bit more stubborn. We were rolling on the floor when Abby came into the classroom.

'Sticky! You promised!'

'They said …'

'I don't care. You know what I said.'

My heart sank. 'You can't mean it.'

'Give me a good reason why not.' She folded her arms.

'There's nowhere to go,' I said desperately.

'There's plenty of spare desks at the back.'

'Everybody will laugh.'

'Let them laugh,' she said, and gave me that aggressive look again.

'Mr Hawkins wouldn't like it.' I'd hit on the right thing to say. It seemed to count with Abby.

She chewed her lip. 'Oh, all right,' she agreed. 'Just this once.'

I didn't want to sit with her when she was bossy like that. The fighting was all for her anyway.

In a rage I grabbed my books. I went to the back and scorched swear words into the desk lid with ugly-vision.

At play time Abby wouldn't talk to me. She was surrounded by girl friends and they hissed like geese when I went near. Rich and me had a real fight. We were sent to the head teacher. She gave me a letter to take home to Mum. What a terrible day.

I raced to the rec and didn't even stop to make traffic jams. They must have thought it was Sunday.

The others strolled up in ones and twos. I tried to get them organised, but we were waiting for Rich and the ball again.

'You took your time.'

Rich wouldn't look at me. 'There were things to sort out,' he said.

'Well, let's get started,' I said. 'Who's going to choose?'

'Danny,' said Rich. Danny smiled. 'And Abby.'

'Hang on, we can't have two captains and I always choose.'

Now Rich looked at me. 'That's it, Sticky,' he said. 'We don't see why you should always choose.'

'Because I'm the best, that's why.'

'But you're only the goalkeeper, and Abby put three past you yesterday.'

'Only the goalkeeper, who says I'm only the goalkeeper?' I was getting into a fighting rage.

'I do, Sticky,' said Abby. 'Are you going to fight me?'

Everyone was against me. It hurt, but I gave in. At least I wouldn't have to wait long to get picked.

I waited, and waited. Players with two left feet were picked while I stood there with my face burning. Didn't they want a goalie? Under my breath I chanted, Choose me, Abby, choose me!

Danny finally picked me. I ran towards the goal –
but John Harrison was already there.

'John wants a go in goal,' said Danny. 'We think
that's fair.'

Fair! It might have been fair, but it wasn't football.
Abby scored whenever she wanted against John
Harrison. At half-time Danny grudgingly put me in
goal. We lost eight two.

School next day was quiet. Nobody talked about
the game. I don't think anyone had enjoyed it. Just
before lunch Mr Hawkins called me to the front.

'What did your mother say about the letter?'

'Letter?'

'The letter, Sticky. The letter the head gave you to
take home yesterday.'

I had forgotten the letter, lost the letter – my mind
was completely blank about letters.

'At lunch, Sticky.' Mr Hawkins spoke with exagger-
ated patience. 'Find-the-letter-at-lunchtime.'

I ran home at the end of morning school. Mum
produced a soggy unreadable mess from the washing
machine. The letter had been in my football kit. I ran
back to school and missed lunch.

When I got to the classroom I was so miserable my
feet wouldn't go to the desk at the back. I looked
round the class. Something had changed. At first I
couldn't see what it was. Then I saw that some of the

boys were talking to girls. Tom was talking to Marie Richards. Rich was talking to Karen Hardy.

It felt like when they used to do what I said, but this time I hadn't said anything. They were copying me and Abby. Perhaps everything would be all right. I hadn't used my fists. Perhaps I wouldn't have to use them any more, much.

The talking stopped. Everyone looked up to see what I would do. For a moment, I thought about giving them all a dose of ugly-vision. The moment passed, and I decided to let them live. I went to where Abby was sitting.

'All right,' I said. 'I'll try. As long as nobody starts anything.'

She smiled and the sun shone again. I sat down beside her.

'But I'm no Prince Charming,' I said.

'Who'd want a boring old prince when they could have a lovely frog like you?' she said.

Then she leaned over and kissed me on the cheek. Everybody cheered.

Wow!

baggy shorts

alan macdonald

And there it is, the final whistle and Ditchley Rovers are through to a Wembley cup final for the first time in their history. The players are dancing around and hugging each other. The crowd (four parents and a kid in a pushchair) is going wild. Joss Porter, Ditchley's goal hero, runs towards the touch line with both arms in the air and salutes his dad. These are amazing scenes!'

I do commentaries like that in my head all the time – at school, on the bus, even underwater in the bath. But this commentary I was doing last Saturday afternoon was different. It was the real thing, I didn't have to make it up. Ditchley Rovers really had just made it through to our first ever Wembley final. And I scored one of the goals. Okay, so the ball bounced in off my knee but that's how I sent their goalkeeper the wrong way. And okay, so the final wasn't at Wembley Stadium, it was at Wembley Park. They're very similar, except the pitch at Wembley Park has hardly any grass and dips in the middle like a banana.

But that didn't matter to me. As I said to our manager the next day, 'We're in the final, that's all that counts.'

'Don't keep saying that, Joss,' said Dad. 'I'm trying to find Stanley Matthews.'

Dad was busy with his cigarette card collection. He's got boxes full of them. Cards he collected when he was a boy with colour pictures of ships, trains and wild birds. The ones I like best are his football cards. Famous players of the past with centre partings and teethy smiles.

Dad found the card he was looking for and held it up to show me.

'Stanley Matthews. The wizard of dribble. Now there was a real footballer. You never saw *him* kissing one of his team mates when he scored a goal.'

I nodded, but I wasn't really listening. All I could think about was Saturday and Ditchley Rovers v Top Valley. It was Top Valley's third cup final in a row. Really there ought to be a rule against teams hogging the cup. It was well known Top Valley creamed off all the best players in the area. Their manager went round all the school matches scouting for new talent. Most of Ditchley Rovers couldn't even get in their school team (me included). But Dad said that wasn't the point – everyone deserves a chance. It's not the winning that counts, it's the taking part. Which was another way of saying Top Valley were going to thrash us 8–0 on Saturday.

'I think it'll be a close game,' I said to Dad.

He didn't answer. Too busy glueing Stanley Matthews into his album.

'I mean the cup final, Dad. We'll probably only win by one goal.'

'It doesn't matter whether you win, Joss, as long as you all play your best.'

'You think we'll lose then? Our own manager doesn't give us a chance.'

'I didn't say that.'

'They're going to bury us, aren't they, Dad?'

Dad sighed heavily. 'Can't you just stop thinking about Saturday for five minutes?'

But I couldn't stop thinking about it. It was the cup final. Ditchley Rovers had never played in a final before and we weren't likely to play in one again. The truth was we were dead lucky to be in the final. There was a flu bug going round and two of the teams we were supposed to play against had to pull out because they couldn't raise a side. In the semi-final our goalie, Flip, made a string of blinding saves and then I scored a late winner with my knee. Dad said that if Eric Cantona had been playing against us that day he probably would have tripped over and sprained his ankle during the warm-up.

The trouble was, now that we were in the cup final I couldn't help it. At school, on the bus, under water in the bath ... I was working on a new commentary.

'And it's all over. Top Valley hang their heads. They can't believe it. Ditchley Rovers – who nobody gave a chance going into this game – have made an amazing comeback. Three goals in three minutes from deadly Joss Porter have turned the game on its head. And now he's being carried shoulder high by the Ditchley team as he lifts the cup to the crowd. The roar is deafening …'

It was all a dream, of course. Top Valley were going to slaughter us.

On Thursday we met for a practice session over at Wembley Park. Dad called us together for a team talk. He was wearing his navy tracksuit with the England 1966 badge on the pocket.

'Now we all know that Saturday is a big game for us. Our Joss has been going to bed with his kit on every night – just to make sure he doesn't miss the kick-off.'

Everyone looked in my direction and laughed. I hated it when Dad made stupid jokes about me. Sometimes I wished he wasn't our manager.

Dad went on. 'A cup final is special. There are plenty of kids who'd like to be in your boots on Saturday. But they're not. It's your chance, so make the most of it.'

I looked around. Matt, Flip, Sammy, Nasser and the rest were nodding their heads seriously. You could see they were as keyed up as I was.

We lined up for shooting practice against Flip.

'Flip me Joss! Why don't you break me fingers or something?' he said as he stopped my shot.

The truth is Flip's not a bad goalie. If it wasn't for him we'd never have reached the final. He's not very big but he isn't afraid of anything. This evening he was in great form, flinging himself down to stop a shot and springing up again like a jack-in-the-box. Hardly anything got past him.

A cold wind blows across Wembley Park on a winter evening. A thin mist drifted over from the river. It was Nasser who noticed the tall kid behind the goal watching us.

'Hey, Joss,' he grinned. 'You seen old baggy shorts over there? Think he wants a game?'

I looked behind the goal. The tall kid was standing to one side of the posts with a ball tucked under his arm. He had a body like a runner bean. Somehow it held up a pair of shorts that came down to his knees and flapped in the wind. He wore a green roll-neck jumper. Above it his big ears stuck out like mug handles under a flat grey cap. The total effect was like a jumble sale on legs.

By now Sammy, Matt, Nasser and the others had noticed him. They started making sniggering comments.

'Clock the gear, eh?'

'Is that Arsenal's away strip?'

'No, must be Oxfam's.'

'Let's sign him on. He can be our secret weapon.'

'Yeah, he can hide the match ball in his shorts.'

Nasser said the last joke too loud because Baggy Shorts frowned and looked at the mud.

'Shut up!' I said. 'He'll hear you.'

A few minutes later I went to get a ball from behind the goal. Baggy Shorts was still standing there with the ball under his arm. The cold didn't seem to bother him. I wondered why he kept watching us.

'Hello,' I said. 'You from round here?'

He touched his cap and nodded seriously. 'Used to be.'

'What happened? Did you move away?'

'Kind of.' There was a pause. 'I'm a goalie,' he said, looking straight at me.

'Are you?'

'Yes. I'm a good goalie.'

'I bet you are. But we've already got a goalie. Flip. He's over there.'

I jerked my head in the direction of the goal. Baggy Shorts nodded again. 'I'm a good goalie,' he repeated, bouncing the ball and catching it in his big pale hands. I noticed it was made of heavy brown leather held together with a lace.

'We're playing here Saturday in the cup final,' I said. 'You can come and watch if you want.'

Baggy Shorts nodded again. 'I never played in a

final. Never.' He looked away into the distance as if there was something just out of sight. The mist had got thicker. I realised I was shivering.

'Well, kick-off's at three.' I said. 'Come and support us. I gotta go now. See you.'

I ran back to the others. The shooting practice had stopped. Everyone was gathered round Flip who was sitting on the ground. Dad was kneeling beside him, looking at his nose which was an ugly swollen red.

'Ah flip me! Don't touch it!' he cried out.

'What happened?' I asked.

'I didn't know he was coming for the cross,' said Sammy. 'I was jumping to head the ball and Flip came out and somehow … I headed him instead.'

'It was my flippin' ball,' moaned Flip. 'I called for it.'

'Will he be all right?' I asked Dad. 'For Saturday, I mean? He will be able to play on Saturday, won't he?'

Dad helped Flip to his feet. 'It's probably just a nasty bruise. But I'll take him to the hospital to get it looked at just in case. The rest of you better go home. It's getting late.'

We trooped miserably off the field.

'Nice one Sammy,' I said. 'If Flip can't play on Saturday there goes our only chance. Without him Top Valley will murder us.'

As we were leaving I remembered Baggy Shorts

again. I turned back to wave goodbye. But he'd gone, melted away into the mist.

It was Cup Final day, and we were sitting in the dressing room in silence, all staring at the floor. Dad had just asked if anyone wanted to play in goal. The news about Flip was bad. The hospital said his nose might be broken; it was hard to tell until the swelling went down. Broken or not, there was no way he could play in a cup final.

We'd have to play our sub, Gormless Gordon, at right back. That meant someone else had to go in goal.

The news was greeted in the dressing room as if someone had died. There was no point in kidding ourselves any longer. We'd lost the final before the game started. I could hear the commentary running through my head:

'And it's another one! This time through the goalkeeper's legs. This is turning into a massacre. 32–0 to Top Valley and there's still half an hour to go! Ditchley Rovers must wish the final whistle would blow and put them out of their misery.'

That's why no one was volunteering to put on the green jersey. The goalkeeper always gets the blame. He's the one the rest of the team picks on when they're losing badly. That's why I couldn't believe it when Dad spoke to me.

'Joss, you've played in goal before.'

I looked up in horror. 'That was only messing around in the park. I've never played in a proper match.'

'There's always a first time. You could do it.'

'Dad! No way! I'm a striker. I'd be hopeless in goal.'

'Well, somebody's got to. Listen all of you, Flip isn't coming. We've just got to put out the best team we can. And if we lose it's no disgrace. Now I'll ask again – is anyone willing to go in goal?'

I looked around at the rest of the team. Pleading with them: *'Not me, anyone but me, somebody else do it, please.'* No one would look at me. They stared at the floorboards as if they wanted to crawl underneath.

'Right, that's it then. Joss, you're in goal first half,' said Dad, losing patience. I picked up the green jersey he threw at me. It wasn't fair. He shouldn't be manager if he was going to pick on me.

Top Valley were already out on the pitch in their smart new kit. Red and white striped shirts with their names on the back. Just like professionals.

'Come on, you Valley kings! You'll murder this lot!' shouted their manager from the touch line. Most of their team were bigger than us. I recognised Gary Spencer who is top scorer for our school team. He gave me a nod.

'Hi Joss! They're not playing you in goal, are they?'

I nodded miserably.

'You *must* be desperate,' he said, rubbing his hands together. You could see him imagining all the goals he was going to score.

The game kicked off. Top Valley sent the ball straight down the wing. We didn't clear it. A high ball came over. I started to come out for it, then changed my mind. As I tried to get back, the ball thumped into the corner of the net. Gary Spencer wheeled away with his arms going like windmills.

'Goooooooooal!'

Nasser shook his head at me in disbelief. 'Why didn't you come out?'

'Why didn't you mark him if you're so great?' I snapped back.

The rest of the first half we defended grimly, hardly ever getting past the halfway line. Top Valley went two up after twenty minutes. After that, I made a few lucky saves and we kept the score down by keeping ten players back and booting the ball anywhere.

As the minutes ticked toward half-time, I noticed the mist drifting in again from the river. I heard a ball bounce behind me and there was Baggy Shorts. He was wearing the same as before – grey cap, green jumper, huge baggy white shorts.

'Hi,' I said. 'Come to watch us get beaten?'

He stood to one side of my goal.

'Where's your goalie?' he asked.

'Broke his nose. Couldn't come. That's why they stuck me in goal.'

He nodded thoughtfully. 'I'm a goalie,' he said.

'Yeah,' I replied, 'you told me that the other day.'

'I'm good.'

'But you don't play for our team.'

'I could do, though.'

Baggy Shorts took off his flat cap and held it in both hands. His hair was cut short over his big ears and parted in the middle. He looked at me, his eyes full of longing.

'Please. I never played in a final. Never. Give me a chance.'

It came out in a rush. Then he put his cap back on and waited.

At that moment the referee blew for half time.

'You must be bonkers, Joss,' said Sammy. 'Look at him. He turns up out of nowhere in his grandma's bloomers and you want to play him in goal.'

'But we haven't got a goalkeeper,' I argued. 'We're going to get beaten anyway. What have we got to lose?'

'Another ten goals,' said Nasser.

I pulled off the green jersey.

'Well, who's going in goal for the second half then? I've done my bit.'

Nobody took the jersey from me. We all looked at

Dad. It was his decision. He stared across at Baggy Shorts who stood a little way off, bouncing his old leather ball.

'Everyone deserves their chance,' said Dad.

Gormless Gordon went off and Baggy Shorts came on as a sub. I could see the Top Valley players grinning as Baggy Shorts took the field. He ran past them, shorts flapping in the wind and cap pulled down over his eyes.

Gary Spencer sidled up to me as we lined up for kick-off.

'Where'd you get him then? On special offer at Tesco's?'

I stared back at him coldly. I'd had enough of being the joke team. If we were going to lose then the least we could do was make a fight of it.

From the kick-off, Sammy passed to me and I burst through the middle. Top Valley were caught half asleep and my pass found Nasser in the penalty area. He shot first time, low into the corner. 2–1.

It was the start we needed to get back in the game. But it also stung Top Valley awake. They soon had the ball back up our end and Gary Spencer carved his way through our defence. He left three players on the ground as he raced into the penalty area.

There was only Baggy Shorts left between him and the goal. Spencer looked up to pick his spot. It was too easy. But in that second, Baggy Shorts came racing off his line like a greyhound and threw himself on the ball. Spencer couldn't take it in. One minute he had the ball, the next Baggy Shorts had whipped it off his boot and kicked it upfield. The small crowd watching clapped. Ditchley Rovers looked at each other in astonishment. Baggy Shorts wasn't just good, he was brilliant.

The rest of the game Top Valley tried to find a way to beat our new goalkeeper. They aimed for the corners. They rained in shots like cannonballs. They tried to dribble round him. But Baggy Shorts was a mind-reader. He seemed to know exactly where the ball was going. He leapt like a cat and pulled it out of the air. He rolled over, sprang to his feet, bounced the ball twice and sent it into orbit. With just ten minutes to go we got a goal back to level the scores at 2–2. Then, as the minutes ticked away, the disaster happened. Gary Spencer went through again and again Baggy Shorts dived at his feet. But this time Spencer was waiting for it. He went sprawling over the goalkeeper and lay in the mud holding his leg.

'Ahh, ref! Penalty!'

Anyone could see it was an obvious dive but the referee blew his whistle and pointed to the spot.

Spencer made a miraculous recovery to take the penalty himself. He winked at Baggy Shorts with a smug grin on his face. Baggy Shorts didn't say a word, he went back on his goal-line. I walked away to the halfway line feeling sick. Three minutes to go and we were going to lose to the worst penalty ever given. But as Spencer placed the ball I couldn't help myself. I always do the commentary for penalties.

'And the crowd are hushed. Baggy Shorts crouches on his line. Spencer takes a run-up. He hits it hard, low, into the corner … it's … No! Baggy Shorts has saved it one-handed. An incredible save! Spencer has his head in his hands. Baggy Shorts gathers the ball. Sends a long kick upfield. Towards … ME! Help! Where is everybody?'

I just kept running towards the goal waiting for someone to tackle me. But nobody did. And as their goalkeeper came out I slipped the ball under his body. It rolled gently over the line. Goal – and this time I hadn't used my knee either.

The whistle went soon after. Ditchley Rovers had won the cup. 3–2 with a dramatic late winner from deadly Joss Porter. Just as I'd predicted all along. I was mobbed by the whole team, jumping on top of me until we were all rolling around in the mud, laughing. Dad was going round banging everybody on the back. I don't think he could quite believe it.

Then we had to line up for the cup to be presented. Sammy said, 'Where's Baggy Shorts? He should go up first. He was man of the match.'

We looked around. But we couldn't find him. No

one knew where he'd gone. I looked back to the goalmouth where he'd saved the penalty, but there was no one there, only a fine mist drifting in from the river.

A few days after the cup final, Dad was working on his cigarette card collection again. I saw him stop with the glue in one hand and a card in the other. He was staring at something.

'What is it?' I asked. He handed me the card in his hand. It was from the football series. On the back it said:

Player number 132: Billy Mackworth. Goalkeeper. Despite his boyish looks, Mackworth was a talented goalkeeper for Spurs. He should have been the youngest player to play at Wembley in the 1947 cup final. Sadly he died in a road accident a few days before the game. He never played in a cup final.

There was no mistaking the picture. He looked older but the two big ears still stuck out like mug handles under his cap. The eyes stared gravely into the distance. It was Baggy Shorts.